RAGDOLL RIPOFF

IRIS LEIGH

Ragdoll Ripoff

A cat may be at the center of a break-in at the library.

I'm Kat Jones and my very first client needs my help to find the person responsible for swapping an ancient book with a fake. As if that isn't baffling enough; where they found the fake is a place no one knew existed.

To solve this case, I'll need to team up with Rusty. What we discover is a treasure trove of secrets that lead to the origin of the book and not who but what four-legged creature may be responsible.

Contents

Chapter 1

Nothing could ruin my week. No random talking cats had popped up and ambushed me out in public; a first in a very long time. The talking felines were still at home, but they were slowly but surely growing on me. It was like having kids. I was getting better at tuning out their nonsense—and cats come with a lot of it. Did you know the texture of a new brand of cat litter could supply a conversation for days? I'd found that out the hard way when their preferred brand had sold out.

Despite the nonsense with the cats, the best part about this week didn't even involve them. Well, everything involved the cats whether I liked it or not, but the highlight of my week, and why I was in such a good mood, was because there were no new cases!

So there I was, skipping down the street, a big grin on my face. I wanted everyone to see how happy I was. With iced coffee in hand, I waved hello to strangers who passed by. I was just enjoying life while I could, knowing it wouldn't last forever. It couldn't. The cats would eventually sink their claws into me and drag me back to solving cases, kicking and screaming. But something would have to transpire in the town before there was anything to solve. That was the true reason I was happy—everything was absolutely and wonderfully normal and boring!

I rounded the corner and took a big sip of my iced coffee. Daniel had put some caramel syrup in it, along with another shot of espresso. After our eventful time in the woods, he had been way more cheery around me, but I was okay with it because it resulted in discounted drinks. Who knew having a near-death experience would be so beneficial? Maybe I should find another person at another shop I would like to frequent and repeat the process. I could just imagine the discounts at the grocery store, department store, or Pete's Pet Supplies. Yeah, the amount of money I was spending at that last place was adding up. Having to take care of two and a half cats was not cheap.

My cheerful mood didn't last as long as my coffee. Detective Davidson was standing in front of the library. Not the biggest cause for concern, but the yellow caution tape wrapped around the front of the building, the crowd of people, and police cars were. I took a few steps forward to see if I could identify what had warranted such a show.

A knot of dread formed in my stomach, and it grew with every step I took. There was one thing in that library which could cause my week to implode. A certain feline that resided there. With his orange coat, he would stick out like a sore thumb if he were out and about. Picking my way through the crowd, I observed Detective Davidson talking to Mr. Tempest. As always, Detective Davidson was scribbling away in his notebook while feverishly nodding his head. Something juicy must have happened.

Oh well, not my problem!

Feeling happy I had successfully appeased my curiosity while also avoiding solving a crime myself, I went home. Or... I tried to. But the saying curiosity killed the cat wouldn't be true if I wasn't stopped before I could make my grand escape. Someone tapped me on the shoulder as I debated whether or not to make a run for it before I got dragged into whatever was unfolding at the library. Surely it wasn't a cat. They couldn't reach that far up, and it had felt more like a human hand than a feline paw. To be on the safe side, I prepared myself to reprimand whichever cat had dared approach me in public firmly, but it wasn't a cat. It was a human. One I knew from a previous case, one who also had a cat.

"Delores Fuller?"

"Good to see you again, Kat," she said with a smile.

"Same to you. I see the library is closed."

"I know. So sad. No new books for me till they reopen."

I nodded. Her last stack should have lasted her a while, but I guess she was a fast reader and had quickly zoomed through them.

"Will you be solving this crime as well?" she asked, nodding toward the library. It wouldn't take a genius to figure out what she was hinting at. It was the only place around with caution tape and police surrounding it. But was I going to solve it?

"Absolutely not!" I happily said. I wouldn't be touching whatever had happened at the library with a ten-foot pole. Not even for a million dollars... Okay, I would do it for a million. They could easily bribe me with money.

"Oh, I just figured that was why you were here." Her lips curved into a frown. Was she sad I wouldn't be the one to figure out what'd happened in the library?

"Nope, a coincidence... Wrong time, wrong place."

"I see... I guess I will just have to wait till the library reopens before I can check out more books."

Yeah, she was sad that I wasn't looking into the incident at the library. She would just have to wait till Detective Davidson put the clues together and got to the bottom of whatever had transpired.

What exactly happened here?

I poked Delores, grabbing her attention again as I asked, "Do you know what actually happened that caused it to close?"

"Some items were stolen."

I cocked my head to the side. Someone had stolen from the library? What was even worthwhile to steal at the library? Maybe some rare, first-edition book. Or a signed copy from an author. But couldn't they have just checked out the book and not returned it? It was a library, after all.

"Uh... couldn't they just check out the item instead of stealing it? What was stolen?"

"I'm not sure, but something is missing."

"Hmm... I wonder what."

I wondered, but I wasn't about to be tempted by that curiosity. It is what killed the cat, after all. I waved goodbye to Delores and made my way home, taking sips of my iced coffee as I went.

Chapter 2

C uriosity didn't kill the cat, it killed the human. Over and over. Despite not having nine lives, the world acted like I did as I spied two cats blocking my front door. It was already too late to pretend I hadn't seen them. We had locked eyes, and they were watching me.

"Well, hello there... Lola and Rusty." I greeted the pair of familiar felines that waited for me to fish my keys out of my pocket and open my front door. "To what do I owe the pleasure of your presence today? Oh, wait, let me guess... the library?" I asked sarcastically. Could cats understand sarcasm? I hoped so.

"Good job, human. Your observation skills have increased!"

Cats didn't understand sarcasm. Or perhaps they did and Lola had just ignored my attempt in favor of annoying me. The latter was a lot more plausible.

"Seriously, Lola? I'm not solving any cases."

"You must. This is a very important case," she purred back as the pair of cats followed me inside. I kicked off my shoes, went to my living room, and promptly collapsed on the couch.

"I'm resting here," Luna said as my presence had rudely awakened her at home. It was payback for all the times they had abruptly jerked me out of my sleep.

"Not sorry," I said to the gray feline, before focusing on the two cats that were about to make my great day a horrible one. "Desperate case here... important case there... It's all the same to me. Regardless of how you classify your cases, I'm sitting this one out."

"You can't. The world depends on you!"

My mind screeched to a halt. The world depended on me? If the world's fate rested in my hands, then the world was doomed. And if the world ended, I wanted to enjoy the time I had left my way. I didn't want to spend it on some mysterious—and no doubt tiresome—journey with talking cats. They needed to find someone else to be the hero of that tale, not drag a girl who just wanted to be lazy into it.

"I'm going to have to pass," I said as I fumbled around on the couch in search of the remote. "Aha!" I located it, pointed it toward the TV and clicked it on as I sank into the couch, ready to get lost in a show and settle in for the night.

"You can't."

"Sure I can, I just did." I raised my almost-finished iced coffee in a toast to my own laziness before taking another sip.

Lola jumped right up on the couch and sat on my stomach, her full weight pressing down on me as her eyes narrowed. She was upset. Regardless of how annoyed she was, she wasn't dragging me into this one. Or the next one. I was hanging up my hat and calling it quits.

"What do you not understand about the world being at stake?"

"Everything, Lola. How does that even make sense? Someone stole something from the library, and now the world is going to end?"

"The world isn't ending."

"Then the world isn't at stake. Problem solved."

"Human…" Lola spoke slowly as she took a step forward.

"Cat…" I said as I held her gaze. I wasn't going down without a fight.

"A precious book is missing. We need you to retrieve it before it falls into the wrong hands."

Book? So it was a book that was stolen. Delores Fuller hadn't known what was taken from the library, but the cats somehow did. My gaze drifted toward Rusty. It had to have been him. He lived at the library, after all.

"Are we talking about some valuable first-edition book? One signed by an author who is long dead? Is it worth millions, even billions?" I asked, thinking surely that had to be the only reason a book could be worth such a fuss.

"No, something much worse."

"What could be much worse? Are we talking, like, summoning demons? If so, magic doesn't exist." I rolled my eyes as I let loose a huff, followed by a fit of giggles. This was the real world we were talking about, after all. But the giggles subsided real quick when Lola didn't talk back. I glanced over at Rusty, who held my stare, never blinking. A familiar knot of dread was back in my stomach.

"Lola, please tell me you're kidding." I spoke slowly, afraid of what was going to spill out of the feline's mouth.

"I told you it's an important case."

"But magic doesn't exist."

Lola shot me a look. I couldn't explain it. My mind was still trying to understand what we were talking about, because surely we weren't saying magic was real.

"You're talking to cats right now, but you don't think magic exists?"
Huh.

Is that how I'd gotten the ability to talk to cats? When I'd been electrocuted, had magic flowed into my body and granted me the ability to talk to them? And, if the book was magical, then that might mean...

I jumped up, causing Lola to tumble down to the floor as I smiled. "Does this book have the ability to get rid of being able to understand cats?"

"No."

I scrunched my face up into a scowl at her quick and short response. "Then I'm not interested." I laid back on the couch, avoiding the feline on the floor.

"You are passing up the chance to touch a book so powerful that humans can't even read it?"

"If I can't read it, then what's the point of finding it?"

"Because it is magical!"

"Well then, sounds like you need to find a witch, not a human... if witches exist." I narrowed my eyes as I leaned over the couch to look at Lola on the ground. "Do witches exist too?"

"You are going off-topic. We must find this book!"

"Hmm... But tell me, if a human can't read the book, why steal it? It's no use to us," I thought aloud as I clicked through the channels, trying to find something that would grab my attention and drown out the voices of those around me.

"Human, we are serious! We must find this book at all costs!"

I paused my channel surfing for long enough to flash Lola another look. The one I received told me she wasn't too happy with me, but she couldn't just go around expecting me to believe the world needed my help! All this talk about how magic exists and that somehow I was the only one who could solve this mysterious book theft was a lot to expect me to believe. But at this rate, and considering how adamant she was about it, I knew I would lose. It was better to cut my losses earlier than later in hopes I would have some quiet time to enjoy.

"Alright. If I solve this case, will you leave me alone for a bit? No cases, nothing."

"Sure," Lola said quickly.

"Well, I guess we've got a deal, then."

Chapter 3

"This might be a bad idea."

"You already agreed," Rusty said in as he sat at my feet. Both of us were looking at the front of the library. It was still taped off. For us to investigate who committed the robbery, I would need access to the crime scene. Mrs. Higgins had drilled that into my head. One could not solve a crime without first establishing and examining where it had happened.

"Are we just going to wait out here?"

"I mean, we can't just walk through the front door."

"Sure we can. I've done it a million times before," Rusty said.

I rolled my eyes. Did he not understand that he was a cat and a crime had just been committed at the library? People would notice a human, not a four-legged feline that could talk to humans, unless they were out of their mind. Which was me. I was the crazy one who could talk to cats.

Glancing up and down the street, I tried to see if anyone was watching me. No one was. People who passed by quickly glanced at the caution tape and then continued on with their business, unaware of what I was about to do. I wasn't even sure exactly what I was going to do myself.

"You have any idea about how to get into the library without going through the front door?" I asked as I bent toward the ground to be closer to Rusty. We didn't want to attract the attention of anyone on the street. Instead, I pretended to be tying my shoes as I undid them and redid them.

"Well, there is the window."

"Seriously? Window again? No back door?"

The last window I'd attempted to crawl through was one at Alec's new home, where Bridget had caught and questioned me. It had put me off windows, that's for sure. If I could stick with doors, I would.

"No back door. Well, there is one, but that's not an option unless you want to set off the alarm."

"Window it is," I muttered, groaning as I stopped tying my shoes for the fourth time and stood up, dusting the dirt off my knee as I walked down the street. When I appeared at the edge of the library, I took another glance around to see if anyone had stopped to watch the crazy girl with a cat, but no one had. So I darted down the side, toward the back of the building.

"Alright, which window?" I asked as I scanned the windows that lined the building to see if any of them were already cracked open so I could easily slip inside. There was to be no breaking of windows or the cops would be on the lookout for two people. And I didn't want to go to jail.

"There is a window that is cracked open in the back left corner of the library."

I had run down the right side of the building, which meant I needed to make my way over to the other side to creep in and find out what was truly going on. Channeling the stealth of a cat, I hurried along the back till I made it to the other side. It was a good thing the back of the library didn't face a street or I would be in trouble. When I arrived on the left side of the building, I scanned the structure, trying to identify the window Rusty was talking about. The windows were slightly smaller on that side, and higher.

"Rusty, which one?" I whispered.

"In the back, the one right next to you," Rusty said as he ran forward, propelling himself onto the building and scaling it easily to land on the ledge. He pawed at the screen to show that it was ripped as he wiggled his body through, pushing the window open before disappearing. That left me completely alone outside. Anyone passing by would think I was odd, and I would've agreed if I could've seen myself as I ran forward in an attempt to mimic the cat's movements. I jumped, my hands only just grabbing hold of the ledge. My body crashed against the brick structure as I felt a sharp jolt of pain course through my body. I cradled my arm. I had body-slammed into the structure way harder than planned. Even though I could talk to cats, I was not as nimble as them. But I had to keep trying.

"What is taking you so long? You just jump!" Rusty growled as he poked his head out from the window he had disappeared into. Just jump. Yeah, as if it was as easy as that. He didn't know it wasn't. Cats had incredible balance and agility. They could fall from incredible heights and still land on their feet. If I were to do the same, I would be dead. So no, it wasn't as simple as just jumping.

But it was still a jump I needed to make.

So, I rubbed my hands together and bounced in place for a moment to warm up my body and psych myself up for it. Then I ran straight for the library, lunging as soon as I felt I was close enough. This time, I was able to successfully grab hold of the ledge. Now all I needed to do was pull my body up and I could climb through. Again, easier said than done for someone who avoided working out. Despite feeling like my arms were wet noodles, I planted my feet on the building and hung there momentarily. With two hesitant steps up the side of the library, my body folded in on itself. If I continued this way, my arms would give out and I would end up on my back, staring up at the sky. Instead, I pulled my body up, my arms shaking in the process as I landed one elbow on the ledge, followed by the other. With both elbows resting and supporting my weight, I was able to kick off the building and tug myself forward so I fell through the window. I crashed down to the ground in a sweaty, panting heap and stared up at the library's ceiling.

"It's not that high of a jump," Rusty purred as he stepped onto my chest to stare down at me. I rolled my eyes before closing them. Next time, I think I'd rather just walk through the front door. Who cared if anyone saw me? It was better to do that than be reminded I should probably work out more than I did.

"We should hurry before someone hears your wheezing."

"I'm not even breathing that hard!" I said as I picked myself up off the ground, forcing Rusty to jump off. What was with cats and their bluntness? Unlike them, I wasn't in the habit of climbing through windows and so, of course, I'd be breathing a little heavier when I actually needed to do it.

"Lead the way," I muttered as I caught my breath. The orange cat before me cast a look in my direction before bouncing off, leaving me with no choice but to follow behind.

"You know where you're going, right?"

"Of course, why wouldn't I?"

I rolled my eyes at Rusty's words. There wasn't supposed to be a downstairs part of the library. It was supposed to be a rumor, but talking cats weren't supposed to exist either. And if one was possible, there was a high probability both were.

"Over here!" he called as he walked behind the checkout counter to the office of Mr. Tempest, who didn't keep it locked.

"It's in here? I see nothing."

"Did you really think it would be out in the open?"

I wasn't sure what I was expecting as I followed behind Rusty. He lifted his paw as he tapped an open area in the office's corner.

"Do you have to go to the bathroom?" I asked as I watched him mess around in the corner. Needing to go to the bathroom while we were breaking in to the library was horrible timing, but something always went wrong when the cats were involved. If this was going to be the extent of it, then I would gladly accept it.

"No, it's here!"

"There's nothing there but carpet."

"Don't you see that the carpet is cut?"

Cut? I bent down and inspected the area Rusty was on.

"Oh, there is something here."

"Did you think I was lying?"

I opted not to respond to the feline as I got on my knees, patting around the cutout square to find where it opened. The carpet didn't look worn. I tried to find a handle I could pop open to expose what hid beneath it.

"Oh, wait, I think I found it!" I said happily as I felt a small indent just big enough to slip a few fingers in and pull up. Something un-latched as I yanked the door open, exposing the darkness below.

"Watch it! You almost squished me!"

I peered over the hatch to see Rusty squeezing his way out from between the wall and the door.

"Sorry, got carried away," I said as I looked down to see the room below. "Why is it so dark?"

"Because you haven't turned the light on," he said as he stepped in front of the door and set his paws on the rungs of a ladder that extended downward before descending.

"What's down there?" I called from above, tilting my head down to see where the orange cat had gone.

"Come on down!"

I pursed my lips as I stared at the ladder that extended down into the darkness. I could see the patch of floor directly below, thanks to the light from the office, but I couldn't see what else could be lurking beyond. Rusty was already down there though, and surely he wouldn't lead me into a trap. What kind of trap existed underneath a library anyway?

"Coming," I muttered under my breath. It wasn't like Rusty was around to hear me, but speaking out loud like that provided me some comfort as I grabbed hold of the ladder. Slowly lowering my body until my feet landed on a step, I made my way into the darkness.

"Does Mr. Tempest climb down this ladder all the time? That's dangerous for his age."

I continued making my way down until I was only a few steps away from the ground.

"He should invest in an actual door instead of this."

"There is a door. It's just locked," Rusty called out as I briefly closed my eyes, blinded by the light that turned on.

"I found the light!"

Slowly, I opened my eyes as I stepped off the ladder and onto solid ground. We had to be quick about searching the bottom floor of the library before others returned. It wouldn't bode well for Mr. Tempest to find me down here.

"Rusty!" I called as I turned around to see what we were dealing with, and my mouth dropped. "What in the world is this place?"

"It's the library."

That was a vast understatement. It was like one of those libraries you saw in movies that held ancient relics of the world. But for all of this to exist in my small town? That seemed impossible. But no matter where I looked, I knew I wasn't dreaming. I didn't dream of libraries often, but this one might just stick with me. Bookcases were lined up in rows, with a walkway running between them that led to a podium in the middle.

"Are you just going to stand there?"

I looked ahead to see Rusty standing at the end of the walkway leading to the podium.

"This kind of library only exists in movies," I said as I stepped forward, brushing my hands against the leatherbound books. Some were obviously well worn, while others had gold foil, showing they were expensive. Maybe even rare.

"What?"

I cast a quick look over at Rusty before going back to admiring the books.

"The movies. You know, the grand secret library where you can find things like Excalibur." I froze as my words echoed in my mind.

Could it be?

I whipped my head around, trying to see if I could find anything other than books around me... like a sword.

"Excalibur?"

"Yeah, the sword that belonged to King Arthur. You know, from Britain," I said as I stepped closer to the orange cat, still on the lookout for anything like it.

"And you think the sword would somehow be in America?"

"What?"

"Why would a sword that isn't from here, be here?"

I scratched my head as I stopped looking around. "Because it's always the first item in the magic libraries," I said as I stopped in front of the orange cat at the podium.

"There is no magic sword here. That doesn't exist."

I gave Rusty a side glance. He wanted me to believe in talking cats and a magic book, but not magical swords? I couldn't believe he wanted me to accept that tidbit of information as unbelievable.

"So, this is the book?" I asked, trying to change the topic before we really got lost focusing on the magic sword and what other magical items did or didn't exist.

"Yes, open it," he said, jumping on the podium. My heart froze as I watched him, waiting for red lasers to turn on and alarms to sound, but nothing happened.

"Huh, I guess this really isn't like the movies."

"What are you talking about now?"

"You know, the red lasers that turn on when someone gets too close to the precious item."

"What? Never mind."

I pursed my lips, ignoring the narrowed eyes of the feline watching me. He was judging me. I could tell.

"If the book is missing, then why is there a book still here?"

"It's a fake."

"How do you know it's a fake?"

"Open it already."

Hesitantly, I picked it up so I could peer inside. Even though Rusty had confirmed there were no lasers about to spring to life and cut through me, there was always the chance it was booby-trapped.

"Why are you moving so slowly?"

"Because something can still go wrong," I said as I finished peeling back the cover flap of the book. Instead of being greeted with words from some mysterious book that had to be hidden in a library in a small town, I was met with a doodle. A doodle of a cat sticking out its tongue.

"Really?"

I turned to Rusty as I watched him nod, his paw coming out to tap the open book.

"See, it's a fake."

"And there's a cat doodle."

"Exactly."

"So, I now need to track down a cat that snuck into the library and stole a book?"

"Don't be ridiculous. We can't carry that heavy book!"

I rested my hands on my hips as I stared at the doodle. It was a good drawing, with a gigantic face and a small body. Not exactly accurate, but it'd be an excellent design for a bobble head. With one eye winking and the other wide open, it stuck out its tongue.

"So you're telling me we have a cat... thief on our hands?"

Nothing in life was simple, especially when cats were involved. A cat didn't sneak into the library and steal a book. Just a human who liked cats.

"So, how do we go about finding this cat thief?"

"I'll leave that up to you," Rusty said as he jumped down from the podium, strutting back to the entrance and out the way we'd come. Closing the fake book, I stared at it momentarily, letting everything sink in. Somehow, I needed to find out who else knew about the secret floor of the library. Who was crazy enough to break in to this place, run off with the real book, and leave a fake one behind?

"Easy," I mumbled as I followed the orange feline out from the secret basement. "Sounds so easy..."

Chapter 4

I stood in line, waiting for Mr. Tempest to be free. Several people had stopped by the library to offer their condolences and support after the break-in. No one could fathom why someone would break in to a library. If only they knew about the basement.

"Kat," Mr. Tempest said as the person he was just talking to waved goodbye and quickly made their escape out of the building.

"Morning! I'm sorry about your missing book."

Mr. Tempest narrowed his eyes as he stepped closer. "Book? No one said anything about a missing book."

Oh.

I guess it wasn't common knowledge then.

"Kat, do you know anything about the book?"

"Book? What book?" I said, doing my best not to sound even more suspicious than I already was.

"Oh! I just figured it was a book since it's a library," I said, a few chuckles escaping thanks to my nerves. Hopefully, he bought my reasoning and left it at that.

"Yes, a book. Makes sense. It's a library, after all..." He turned around to walk to the counter.

"I wouldn't be surprised if someone found a rare or signed copy, and that's why they broke in," I said with another nervous chuckle as I followed him. Mr. Tempest tossed a weird look over his shoulder as he raised his eyebrow. I should have just left it alone at the first statement, but I just had to add more. Nerves made you do that kind of thing.

"Kat, do you know something?"

I pursed my lips, leaning on the counter before relaxing my face. I knew something, but he didn't need to know I did. All he needed to know was that I was here and ready to help.

"I'm going to look into the break-in."

I avoided his gaze, as I knew he was looking to see what was truly going on. But I couldn't tell him I had struck a deal with a feline to solve this last mystery in exchange for my freedom. Find this cat thief and the cats would leave me alone. I needed Mr. Tempest to trust me in order for him to tell me everything.

"Can you tell me what happened the day of the break-in? Was there anything—or anyone—suspicious? Perhaps someone in the library who shouldn't have been?"

"Everyone is allowed in the library," Mr. Tempest said as he typed something on the computer at his desk. "But, come to think of it, there was something..."

I leaned in further, urging him to continue so I could figure out who had stolen the book.

"Never mind," he grumbled as he turned around and began messing with some papers, a frown on his face.

"I won't be able to find out who did it if I don't even know where to start," I muttered, hoping he would change his mind and tell me his thoughts about who might have done this.

"This drunk guy kept asking when he could move in."

"Move in? To a library?" I asked, confused. Who would think there were rooms available here to rent that would allow them to move in? Unless they were thinking of crashing on the furniture in the lobby. "Someone wanted to move in here? Why did they think that was possible?"

"No idea."

"Do you know who it was? Or can you at least describe them?"

Finding a drunk man was going to be hard. Finding one who thought the library could be lived in would be even harder. It would be easy to track down a drunk man, but finding the correct one would be impossible. With enough alcohol in their system, a drunk person would confess to anything, even breaking in to a library. I rubbed my temples. It was an impossible task.

"Well, he was wearing a chef's coat."

That was important information. There was one place I could already mark off my list: *Sips of Temptation*. They opted for a button-down shirt as a lure.

"Well, it was black, and had the symbol of a grill on it."

I snapped my fingers as I thought about the restaurants in town. There weren't too many. *Sips of Temptation* was the most popular place in town, but it was a cafe that mostly focused on drinks but served food as well. It wasn't exactly what I would call a restaurant that people made plans to go to for dinner. That would be *Gregory's Grill*. And, if I wasn't mistaken, they used a grill as part of their logo.

"You think it was someone from *Gregory's Grill*?"

"Perhaps, unless they were from out of town."

I nodded at his words. Maybe he was describing someone from out of town. Why else would they think the library was a place to move into?

"Anyone else, or was it just that guy?"

"Well..."

"There is another? What did they do, and what did they look like?"

"There was Mrs. Lawrence."

Mrs. Lawrence?

That name did not ring a bell.

"Who is Mrs. Lawrence?"

"Someone who gets upset easily. She isn't happy about Rusty living here."

I pursed my lips, trying to think of a lady who would have a problem with a cat. But the only person I'd had a run in with that got that easily annoyed was someone around Mrs. Higgins' age, but she had a cat too. If she had a cat, why would she have an issue with Rusty?

"Mrs. Lawrence is the one who also has a cat, right?"

"Yes. Delores's neighbor."

Ah. Now that made sense. Delores lived in an excellent area of town, but it wasn't like there truly was a bad part of town. Though that was something that might be up for debate with the recently increased crime rate. But Delores came from money. Her home, especially the furniture, showed that. It would only make sense for someone else on the block to have money as well. Nowhere near the amount Delores or Alec had, since all the money he inherited.

"Well, I'll add her to my list. Anyone else?" I asked, hoping it would just be two people to question. It would make this both the simplest case of my life and the quickest one if there were only two people to question.

"There are two others."

"Two?"

If there were two others, then that made four possible suspects I would have to track down and question! Four was a lot to do on my own. I nibbled at my bottom lip and crossed my arms over my chest. In order to do this quickly, I may have to enlist the help of some four-legged creatures. But they were also the reason I was solving this case in the first place, and they hadn't been that much help in the last case. I'd ended up needing a human's help with that one... Daniel's help, to be exact. And after what had happened in the forest, I didn't think he would be eager to solve another case with me soon.

"Can you describe the other two?"

The sooner I gathered information on the additional people that would require questioning, the sooner I could be on my merry way to closing this case.

"There was one young gentleman. He has been coming in daily to read a book."

I furrowed my eyebrows at his response. Was it that odd that someone was reading at the library? "I don't understand."

"I had never seen him before, but he insists he has lived in town for several years."

"And all he does is read a book?"

"Yes, one a day."

I frowned. I still didn't understand what was odd about that. "And... that's suspicious?"

"Yes." Mr. Tempest leaned in as he whispered in my ear. "He keeps going on about finding the true meaning of life."

That was weird. The true meaning of life was a question everyone thought of, but everyone had a different answer for. It was perfectly possible for the man Mr. Tempest was describing to find the true meaning of life, but now I was curious about what he thought that was.

"Did he say what he discovered?"

"Nope. He was pretty tight-lipped."

Now I could see why Mr. Tempest suspected the person. How could someone have claimed to have the answer to the hardest question, and not share it with the man who spent his day caring for books with endless knowledge? He would want to know if we'd missed something, and he would want to know if the answer was in his library. It was like a gas station, where they excitedly claimed that they'd purchased the winning lottery ticket at their location. It was a badge to wear with pride to help attract more business. And nothing would gather more business than the meaning of life! Well, the hidden basement floor might if people knew what it contained.

"And the other?"

"Thomas."

I grimaced at the last name. Thomas was a simple person to find. I just wasn't sure whether I wanted to find him. He had dated Bethany in high school and had never grown out of that personality of being a popular kid. He was stuck in the past, and talking to him was irritating. Given the chance, he would rub it in anyone's face that they were less popular than him. I was no different. And now I would have to track him down and ask him if he was the one who broke into the library. I snorted at the thought. Thomas and a library? That didn't go together at all.

"And that's it?" I asked, focusing back on Mr. Tempest and pushing thoughts of Thomas to the back of my mind. That was something I would have to deal with at a later time.

"Yes."

"Well, thank you for the information, Mr. Tempest." I knocked on the counter lightly as I turned away to head toward the front door. "I look forward to solving this case."

That was a lie. I was just looking forward to it actually being solved so I could go back to sitting on my couch and enjoying my life without talking cats ruining it.

Chapter 5

No matter what day of the week it was, *Gregory's Grill* was always busy. Tonight was no different. Several groups were standing outside, waiting to be seated in the small establishment that could only fit so many people without breaking fire code. I nibbled on my bottom lip. It would be hard to question the person Mr. Tempest had seen if everyone was busy. There was nothing worse than trying to stop someone from doing their work during rush hour to ask questions that had nothing to do with what they were doing right then and there. I could already see the raised eyebrows and annoyed grunts when I walked in and asked to talk to someone who worked in the kitchen, likes to drink, and might have tried to move into the library. A snort escaped. I didn't even have the name of the person I was trying to find!

"Do people like the food here that much?" a man groaned. He popped his head around the corner, a cigarette in one hand, and watched the people standing in front of the door. I paused as I scanned him up and down, standing in the shadows of the building that camouflaged him from view. He might have blended in, if only his bright blond hair didn't stick out like a sore thumb. He ran his fingers through his hair and brought the cigarette up to his lips. The white embroidery on his shirt flashed in my direction as he pivoted his body to lean on the building. He was too far away to make out the lettering on the shirt, but there was no mistaking the icon that was present. A grill. An image that *Gregory's Grill* used for their branding.

Surely, it can't be...

I rested my hands on my hips. Had I somehow gotten lucky and stumbled upon a cook taking a break? Joy spread through me at not having to butt my way through the crowd to ask the host if I could talk to someone in the back. Changing my course from heading to the front door to the side of the building, I walked over with a little extra pep in my step. I needed to ask him fast before his break ended.

"And I work a double tomorrow. This is going to suck," he grumbled as he tilted his head back, closing his eyes.

"Excuse me, I have a question."

"I'm on break. You're going to have to ask someone inside."

"Oh, it's not about the restaurant."

He pushed off the wall, opening both eyes as he looked me up and down.

"I don't think I know you."

"Probably not," I said. I had no reason to believe he was lying, unless he'd heard talks of a crazy cat lady who was solving cases. I hoped he hadn't. That would make this conversation a lot more difficult. "But that's okay! We don't have to know each other for the questions I have."

"Look," he said as he crossed his arms over his chest, "I'm not interested in anything you're trying to sell me on. Especially no multi-level marketing scam."

I craned my head to the side at his words. Did he think I was trying to recruit him for something? I cupped my chin as I glanced down at what I was wearing. Everything was what I considered normal, but maybe he just got the vibe I was trying to rope him into something. There was one thing I wish I could unload on him, though. The ability to talk to cats. I would gladly try to get him to take my place. But alas, that wasn't going to happen anytime soon. The ability to talk to cats had magically been bestowed on me after getting electrocuted when I'd plugged in my toaster. And convincing someone else to do that on the small chance they also gained this wonderful but cursed ability would wind up with me in jail. If I was in jail, my peaceful life would be no more.

"Ah, I'm not trying to recruit you for anything," I said as he raised his eyebrows but stayed quiet, waiting for me to respond. "It's just that Mr. Tempest from the library was talking about this place."

"Oh, man... it was one mistake," he groaned as he dropped his cigarette on the ground before squashing it with his shoe. "I swear I didn't mean to make a fool of myself."

"Oh, that was you..." I said, hoping he would keep talking.

"Does everyone know I did that? They will never let me live it down."

"I don't think so?"

"I get really drunk after shifts, and sometimes do things that are a little crazy," he grumbled as he dug his hands into his pockets.

"Kat!" someone yelled, drawing both of our attention to someone waving as they approached us. "Trent, it's good to see you! Working tonight like always?" Daniel asked as he grabbed the guy's hand for a quick shake.

"Gotta make money somehow, ya know?" The man I had been talking to, now identified as Trent, responded as he smiled. "Came out to eat?"

"Of course."

I stood still as I watched the exchange between the two men. They were familiar with each other, friends probably; at least acquaintances.

"Do you two know each other?" I asked.

"Of course," Daniel said as he glanced in Trent's direction before settling his gaze on me, eyebrow raised. "We both work in the restaurant industry."

"So, that means you know each other?"

"For some reason, people in the restaurant industry always flock to the same places regardless of where we work."

Trent laughed as he jabbed Daniel's shoulder before wrapping his arm around him so they were pressed against each other. The height difference between them wasn't huge, but Trent did stand at least a head taller than Daniel.

"And you haven't been coming out lately for some reason... that because you got something else to occupy your time?" Trent said as he jerked his attention my way, smiling at me. I wasn't sure what he meant, but Daniel and I had been hanging out a bit more often. The memory of solving the last case with his help popped into my mind, including the part where I had to save him. The mere thought of that moment had me chuckling, which I tried to muffle.

"Oh, so it looks to be true. Congratulations man, it was about time."

"It's not what you think," Daniel said as he pushed away from Trent, looking everywhere but at us. "What are you both doing out here?" he asked, changing the topic. I guessed he was no longer interested in being the center of attention.

"She was just asking me some questions, nothing you have to be worried about."

"Questions about what?" Daniel asked, finally looking in my direction as he raised his eyebrow. No doubt he was curious to see if I would elaborate on why I was standing at the side of the building, partially in the dark, questioning his friends. I let loose a small huff. He should already know why. Solving cases was taking over my life and, if that wasn't, the talking cats were. It was all I seemed to do lately.

"Just some stuff that concerns the library."

"This wouldn't happen to relate to the break-in, would it? Are you working on another case, Kat?"

Trent stood up straighter as his eyes narrowed at me. "Case? What case? Are the police involved because of me being drunk?" He let loose a deep sigh as he ran his fingers through his loose locks. "My life is really a mess."

"The police are involved with the break-in, yes, but you being drunk is different."

Or at least I think it is.

There was a chance the man before me was the one who'd broken into the library to steal a book, but who knows what was discussed once alcohol was involved? They might have been sharing information I didn't even know existed.

"That's good. Don't need to be adding that to my rap sheet!"

Rap sheet?

I raised my eyebrows in surprise at his words. Trent had a history, but that didn't mean he was the one who'd broken into the library. Although it was also oddly convenient that he happened to show up so close to when a book went missing.

"By rap sheet, what do you mean?" I asked, keeping my tone light and breezy so it didn't seem like I was prying into his business. Nope, not me. I was just a girl interested in learning more about him. He didn't bite, and visibly tensed up.

"Sorry, that information is locked and sealed away. But really, I had nothing to do with what happened at the library. I just like to drink a little too much after work to de-stress. That's it."

"I understand, but maybe..." Just then, a head popped out from behind the restaurant building, looking around before locking on Trent. Without wasting a moment, he yelled out that they'd gotten a big table and needed help.

"Sorry, I gotta go. It was nice talking to you both. Will you be out tonight, Daniel?" he asked as he turned on his heels and jogged to the back of the building, no doubt to enter the establishment through the back door.

"Maybe! I'll see!" Daniel called back as Trent gave a final wave goodbye before disappearing out of sight. With my suspicion gone, I turned to the only other person still around that I could question.

"If you have no plans, do you want to join me for a meal?" Daniel asked. "What?" he said as he tilted his head to the side when he noticed I was already focusing on him.

"Do you know Trent well? Like, really well?"

"I mean, well enough, I guess."

That would have to do for now, because there was no way I was making my way into the kitchen to question Trent during a rush.

"Do you think it would be possible for him to break in to a library?"

"Who, Trent? No way."

"Why do you say that?" I asked, curious about him being so quick to deny that his friend might have the capacity to do such a thing.

"I mean... Trent doesn't read. What's he going to do with a book?"

"Just because someone doesn't read doesn't mean they can't find a use for a book," I said as I thought about his response. One didn't have to know how to read to visit the library and want a book. In fact, Trent not being a reader may just give him the perfect cover and meant no one would suspect him.

"Really, I don't think Trent would steal a book, of all things," Daniel said. I nibbled on my bottom lip as I thought about what to do. Normally, he might be right. But this wasn't just a random book someone could find. It was special. At least it was special to the cats and special enough to the Tempest family to keep it locked up in a basement away from wandering eyes.

"I guess so," I mumbled as Daniel ushered me toward the front door of *Gregory's Grill*, giving me no choice but to join him for a meal. Maybe sticking around for a bit longer would do me good. It'd give me a chance to figure out more about Trent. Taking Daniel's word about his friend not being guilty wasn't something I could afford to do. Not after last time when the culprit of a crime had been standing right beside him.

Chapter 6

I sat on the steps outside the library, watching people walk by like everything was normal. Like just a few days ago there hadn't been a break-in at this very building. Crime was becoming normal in this town. I leaned back, resting my elbows on the concrete as I let loose a deep sigh. It had all started with the talking cats and worsened from there. Solve one case, and two more popped up. A never-ending cycle I had somehow found myself stuck in, with no way out.

"Are you going in?"

I turned to the side to see Delores Fuller standing on the sidewalk with a stack of books in her hands, no doubt on her way to return the ones she had previously borrowed.

"No, I'm trying to find someone."

"Who?"

Now that was a question I wish I could answer. I wasn't sure who exactly I was looking for. All I knew was that they spent a lot of time at the library reading books, and that they talked about finding the meaning of life in one book tucked away in the building behind me. I figured he would show up if I sat in front of the library long enough.

Culprits had a habit of returning to the scene of the crime. So, all I had to do was be patient and wait.

"Not sure, but I'm sure I'll know when I see them."

"Okay," Delores said as she walked past me, climbing the stairs slowly so as not to trip with all those books in hand as she made her way to the library's front doors. With no other words exchanged between us, she entered the building and left me alone on the steps. Once more, I relaxed against the concrete and went back to people watching. He would have to enter the library eventually. When he did, I would be here.

Or not, I thought, as the sun got lower in the sky. It would soon set. My grand plan of waiting in front of the library had been a bust. No one was interested in the building. Only Delores and a group of young girls had entered the building. No one even glanced in its direction as everyone went on with their business.

"This was a bad idea," I muttered as I dropped my shoulders in defeat.

"You're still out here?"

I turned to the voice above me, instantly identifying who had walked out of the library. Delores Fuller. I had stayed outside long enough to see her arrive with one stack of books and leave with a new stack.

"Seems like it."

"The person didn't show up?"

"No," I said as I stood. There was no point in continuing to wait outside. I would need to draft a new game plan to track down the mysterious man who'd somehow figured out the meaning of life.

"Who are you waiting for?"

I scrunched my nose. It was odd to see her so interested in what I was doing, but since it involved the library, it was understandable.

After all, she probably spent as much time in the library as the guy I was trying to track down did.

Wait...

Delores spent a lot of her time browsing the shelves for books. There was no way she hadn't come across another person who spent as much time as she did there.

"Delores!" I squealed with delight as I bounced up the remaining steps to her. She took a step back in shock, but didn't run away. That was a good sign. It wouldn't do to scare off my potential lead.

"Yes?"

"Oh, Delores!" I said as I smiled from ear to ear. "Have you met any strange men at the library lately?"

"What?!"

Her voice came out higher than normal, her cheeks reddening as she refused to meet my gaze. "Why would you say that?"

I gave Delores an odd look. Why was she blushing? It was a simple question.

Oh... did she think I was inquiring about her dating life?

"Oh no, not like that. I'm actually looking for someone who is strange."

"Strange?"

"Yeah, I was told he talks about the meaning of life a lot."

"The meaning of life?"

"That was all Mr. Tempest could tell me."

Delores nodded her head, her stack of books wobbling with the movement.

"I know him."

"You do!"

"Yes, that's Harrison. He's planning a big surprise, so he's been at the flower shop lately."

I could have hugged Delores with how excited I was, but couldn't unless I wanted to send her stack of books tumbling down to the ground. So I settled for a smile and a thumbs up. After spending most of my day at the library, I needed to head to the flower shop before it closed.

"Thank you, Delores! You're a lifesaver!"

I waved goodbye as I ran down the street to Lucy Walker's flower shop. It had been a while since I'd last stepped foot in that place—not since the fiasco with Ms. Hasting's death—but I had seen Lucy around. She was a frequent attendee of the gossip ring with Mrs. Higgins.

It didn't take long to arrive. The open sign was still on display, and the light was still on as Lucy made her way down the spiral staircase to the main floor.

"Afternoon!" I called as I entered, triggering the bell above the door to ring.

"Kat!"

Lucy wasn't the most talkative, at least not compared to the others in the gossip ring, but if she was around a cup of tea, flowers, and in her shop, she had no problem opening up on a few things. She had been immensely helpful during my last case, and I hoped to count on her again for this one.

"I know you close soon, but would you be able to help me out with something real quick?"

"Of course, your case?"

I paused, with my eyebrows raised to the sky as I took in her words. How did she know I was working on a case? The cats couldn't have told her, and I could count the number of humans who knew about it on one hand.

"How do you know about that?"

"April was talking about."

Mrs. Higgins was talking about me? That I could understand, but it still didn't explain how both of them knew I was working on this case. I cupped my chin as I thought about who might have told them. Mr. Tempest and Mrs. Higgins got along great, so I wouldn't be surprised if it had been him. Then there was Daniel. He would tell Mrs. Higgins anything. She had a way of getting information out of people, regardless of whether they wanted to share it.

"I see... and has she said anything else about the case?"

"Nothing other than her protégé is coming along nicely."

Protégé?

My shoulders sagged, and my mouth dropped at the answer Lucy provided me. There was no way Mrs. Higgins was going around telling people I was her protégé! I fiddled with my hair as I silently screamed. First, Lola had told the other cats that I was open to working cases. And now, with my neighbor leading the gossip ring in town, it would be only a matter of time before the whole town came to me with their problems. Then there truly would be no escaping this. Cats and humans would be seeking me out. Would my life ever be peaceful again?

"Kat, are you okay? You look a little flushed."

"Uh-huh..." I mumbled. "Yeah." I tried to calm myself down. "Just peachy."

I needed to focus on the task at hand. Mrs. Higgins would have to be dealt with at a later time. I had to take care of the cat problem first, then I could take care of the human problem.

"Right! I'm looking for someone."

I stepped forward as I inspected the bouquet on the center display. There were several on the table, but the largest one by far grabbed my attention. She'd included every single color of the rainbow in it, and it was radiant.

"Harrison, I'm looking for a Harrison," I said as I cupped a flower. The soft petals felt wonderful against my skin as I inspected the flower next to it. It was a fake flower, one folded out of paper. Tiny words were sprawled across the paper, neatly folded to mimic real flowers.

"This is pretty."

It was an understatement. It was gorgeous. If I ever ordered flowers, I would order an exact copy.

"Sorry I'm late!" a man yelled as he pushed his way into the shop, causing the bell above the door to swing wildly. "Is it ready? I hope so. I can't wait any longer."

Lucy nodded to the man before focusing on me.

"Kat, this is Harrison."

"Hello," Harrison said as he picked up the flowers. "It looks amazing! You did a wonderful job! She's absolutely going to love it!"

Harrison was inspecting the flowers, nodding furiously with every touch. Whoever received those flowers was going to be one lucky girl. But she would have to wait. I needed information on my case from him before he made his grand escape.

"Harrison, you must be a big fan of books." I nodded to the flowers made of book pages as I leaned on the table. I was trying to act casual, not alert him that I was about to interrogate him.

"I wasn't at first, but I have fallen in love with the written word."

So, his obsession with books was a recent thing. That certainly aligned with what Mr. Tempest had mentioned when describing the man.

"I actually just came from the library."

That grabbed his attention as he perked up. "It's back open? So soon, too. I thought they would be closed longer."

"It was a theft. They didn't vandalize anything."

"Still... to think someone would have ill intention toward the library is unheard of." He tucked the flowers into the crook of his arm as he settled his gaze on me, his green eyes lighting up with glee as he smiled from ear to ear. "Can I tell you something?"

Now that was what I wanted to hear. People volunteering information was so much easier. I was all ears for whatever he wanted to tell me. If he wanted to confess to stealing the book from the basement, I would gleefully take that information to the police and close out my case.

"Of course."

From the corner of my gaze, I watched Lucy walk to the counter to grab some ribbon before making her way back to the center display.

"The true meaning of life is being able to snuggle up with your significant other and read books!" Harrison exclaimed as he nodded furiously, like he had just shared the biggest secret. I'm sure, in his mind, he had. I was confused. That was the meaning of life?

"I would always get into arguments with my girlfriend about her reading habits. I just never understood. I mean, like, what was so great about having your face stuck in a book all day when there was an entire world out there to see?"

I stared at Harrison, who had a faraway look in his eyes. He was physically there, but mentally somewhere else as he told me how he'd come to his version of the meaning of life.

"We broke up because of it, but then I thought, let me see..." He glanced down at the flowers touching the book petals. "Let me see why she loved it so much, and now I understand."

He thrust the flowers in my direction, showcasing the beautiful arrangement.

"Our time on Earth is limited, and while I still plan to travel the world with her, we can't do that forever. Something is bound to happen; injury, age, even war. But you know what is forever? Stories."

He hugged the flowers to his chest.

"Every book I can imagine her and I in it."

"So, you live a thousand lives together," Lucy said as she leaned in and wrapped a ribbon around the base of the flowers still held in Harrison's hands.

"Exactly! Sometimes we get mad at each other for things the other did in a book, but we also love each other so much more because of things we did in our other lives."

Harrison lifted the bouquet in the air as he inspected it in every way possible.

"And they are perfect! I'm proposing tonight."

Harrison fished out a credit card from his pocket and handed it over to Lucy, who walked back to the counter to process his payment. All the while, I stared at the man next to me. His love for his significant other and his passion for books were almost palpable. Mrs. Higgins always told me to rule no one out in a crime. That everyone was a suspect till the real criminal was caught. But I was making an exception this time. I was marking Harrison off my list. There was no way this man, with such a profound love for books, would break in to a library. If there was a chance my hasty decision came back to be proven wrong, and he turned out to be the person who'd done it, the world was doomed.

Chapter 7

I stuffed my hands into the pockets of my pants. What Harrison had shared with me was still weighing heavily on my mind. He was so in love that it was crazy to see. To even think someone could be so enamored with someone else that they would want to live a thousand lives with their significant other was almost insane.

I shuffled my feet, frowning as I stared down at the ground. Was what Harrison had with her possible for me? Would I be able to find someone to love me that way?

Impossible.

There was no way I could explain how I could talk with cats to another person. They would think I was a crazy cat lady. And the talking cats was just the start of it...

Cases.

The never-ending cases that Luna had been signing me up for were another thing that would be hard to explain. If someone told me they were taking orders from a talking cat to investigate burglaries, murders, and whatever other crimes transpired, I would laugh in their face. I certainly wouldn't marry them.

But I couldn't laugh. This was my life, and it wouldn't change soon.

"Hi, I'm Kat, and I understand cats..." I mumbled under my breath as I glanced up in shock to see a man with his nose buried in a book on a collision course with me. There was no way we could pivot to avoid crashing into each other.

"Woah!" I said as he glanced up, his body crashing straight into mine, sending me straight to the ground. He was taller and heavier than me. Our collision course did nothing to him except force him to drop his book while I was left picking myself up off the ground.

"I'm sorry! I didn't see you down there."

I looked up at the man, something I had to do even when standing.

"Right..." I muttered as I sidestepped around him, his face instantly familiar to me.

"Uh, excuse me?"

"Yes?" I said, raising my eyebrow. Hopefully, he wouldn't be making another height comment. There was only so much someone could take.

"Kat, right?"

I grimaced at his words. "Yes, Thomas."

He smiled from ear to ear as he nodded his head, no doubt pleased I remembered him.

"I haven't run into you in a while."

We didn't hang around in the same crowd or area. Despite the town being small, it was still possible to avoid someone. Especially if they had the exact opposite interests. And Thomas and I were opposites.

"Probably because we don't like the same things."

"Ah!" he said as he reached out, knocking his fist into my shoulder playfully, causing me to stagger back a few steps from the force.

Did he not know how much taller and stronger he was than me?

Slowly, I reached up and rubbed at my shoulder, doing my best to soothe the throbbing that was starting to increase.

"Everyone loves the gym!"

Everyone does not.

The smile on his face died down as he glanced down at his feet before settling on my face.

"When was the last time you talked to Bethany?"

Now that was confusing. If Thomas spent as much time at the gym as I thought he did, then surely there would be no way for him to avoid running into someone who works there. Setting my hands on my hips, my gaze narrowed as I took him in. Why ask me that question when his chances of running into her far outweighed mine?

"Why?"

"I'm just curious."

I leaned in forward, almost smashing my nose into his chest as I took him in. Surely, he knew that was a very vague response. One I wouldn't let slide. Working on cases made me inquire more into the why and how of what people were doing. And Thomas might not know it, but Mr. Tempest had listed him as someone of interest.

"Curious about what?"

"Just how she's doing, you know?" He sighed as he looked away. "We haven't talked since I got a girlfriend."

Was he curious about what was going on with Bethany because he was still in love with her? Surely, he had to know that cheating in a small town would not stay under the radar. It would spread around town like wildfire, causing his newfound relationship to fail.

"No, I haven't talked to her recently."

It was the truth. Last time I'd had an actual conversation with her, other than in passing, was when we were dealing with a guy who'd been obsessed with her. Despite the tense situation, it wasn't one to be bonding over. I was a little busy fighting crime and trying to get the cats to not out me as a crazy person.

"Ah, okay. No problem. If you find out how she's doing, I wouldn't mind getting an update."

That would not be happening anytime soon.

"By the way." Thomas reached for his back pocket as he pulled out an open book that had been stuffed back there. "You know where I can find this?" He pointed to the book.

"Find what? Another copy?" I asked, confused.

"No, where this is hidden."

"What?" I asked, still not understanding.

Thomas let loose a sigh as he snapped the book shut. "It's a treasure hunt." He showed me the cover with a big American flag and a giant black X on it. It sure looked like a treasure hunt book.

"Supposedly, they hid something away that could bring someone millions." He looked around before lowering his voice once more. "Maybe billions."

Billions.

That was a magic word for me. It invoked so many feelings. To think there was a book out there that would let random people come into billions if they had the lucky chance of being the one to find the hidden treasure it pointed to. But I knew better. Those books were scams. They thrived on people getting enthralled by the hunt to the point they couldn't risk not taking a chance. This would cause everyone to buy the books based on a slim chance of being that lucky person. But not everyone could be lucky enough to fall into billions unless they were Alec Ford. He'd been one of the luckiest people in this world to have been granted so much money. If Alec had all the luck in the world, then I had what was left over. How else could one describe being able to talk to cats?

"Another billionaire in town? Impossible."

"Exactly! And that's why I need to find where the treasure is hidden!" He flipped open the book again to where he had been before, pointing to the paragraph he had asked me about earlier. This time, I leaned in and read the passage.

Once.

Twice.

Three times.

And all of it went over my head.

"Huh?" I huffed as I leaned back and crossed my arms over my chest. Maybe I wasn't cut out to be a detective if I couldn't even crack a riddle. I cupped my chin as I pondered it. If anyone were able to find where the treasure was hidden in town, it would be Mrs. Higgins. She knew everything that happened here, and I wouldn't be surprised if she already knew about the treasure hunt.

"Sorry I can't be of any help. I honestly have no idea what the riddle is talking about."

"No way... I thought you were smart."

Thomas might not have been keeping count, but I sure was. This was the second time he had insulted me. First my height, and now my brains. I dropped my arms to my side, waiting to see if he would say anything else. If he was going to want my help with anything, he had to know insulting me wasn't the best way to go about getting it.

"If you don't know, then I guess I'm doomed."

Thomas turned the book over in his hands. His gaze was fixed on it, completely forgetting I was standing before him.

"I'm sure someone can figure it out."

"Like who? I already searched the library."

I perked up at those words. Thomas had searched the library? By chance, did that also mean he had stumbled onto the hidden floor and found the forbidden book?

"Library?" I asked, my voice croaking in the process. I rubbed my throat, trying to cover up the indication of my sudden interest. One never wanted to let the suspect know they may be onto them.

"Yeah. Nothing in there could help me solve this riddle either."

Thomas placed the book in his back pocket as he rubbed at the bridge of his nose. "Mr. Tempest didn't know either."

He must have pestered Mr. Tempest about the riddle enough to get listed as a suspect. I couldn't blame the librarian for thinking he was suspicious. Someone rambling about finding a hidden treasure and then the secret item in the basement disappearing like that... it was all too suspicious.

"I actually know someone who might be able to help you."

Thomas perked up at my words. I smiled. I might not solve the riddle of the treasure book, but I was still new to solving mysteries. Luckily, an expert in town also happened to be married to a retired police detective. If Mrs. Higgins couldn't figure it out, she could easily convince her husband to help.

"Visit Mrs. Higgins and see if she can help you."

"Here?" Thomas grimaced as he stepped back. "If I let her in on the treasure hunt, she'll probably want a cut."

I shrugged my shoulders. "Better to lose a part than to lose all of it."

Thomas stood there, staring at me a moment before letting out a deep sigh. He sidestepped me, walking past.

"Thanks, Kat! Next time you see me, I'm going to be a billionaire!"

I raised my eyebrows at his excited tone as I watched his back. I highly doubted he would be the first person to find the prize, but one could dream. Just like how I dreamed about not understanding cats anymore.

Chapter 8

I stared at the building I had ended up at. My feet had gone on autopilot and taken me to a destination I was starting to spend a lot of time at.

The library.

Going ahead and climbing the steps of the building, I made my way into the library. It wouldn't hurt to see if anything had happened since I'd last been here. But instantly, I regretted my decision. As soon as I swung the door open, chatter hit my ears.

The noise unfolding was way too loud for it to be happening in the library. But why was it so loud?

Curiosity got the best of me. Maybe it was all the time I was spending around the cats, but I couldn't help but creep forward. It was easy to tell Mr. Tempest was one person in the conversation, but who was the other?

"Oh, Kat!"

I froze. My sneaking into the library had failed. I wasn't as nimble as a cat and surely wasn't as small as one. Of course, Mr. Tempest standing behind the front desk would see me enter the building.

"Kat, come on over!" He waved me over enthusiastically.

"Kat, this is Mrs. Lawrence." He waved to the lady in front of him, who turned around to look at me. Instantly, I froze from the heated look in her eyes. I had walked into hot lava by entering the library, and now that she had her sights on me, there would be no escape without getting burned. "Mrs. Lawrence, this is Kat."

"So you are the one who thought it was a bright idea to give a library a cat?"

"Excuse me?" I said, completely thrown by her words. She had jumped straight to the point. I didn't even know how to react.

"You gave away your orange cat to the library."

"I didn't have an orange cat."

"Oh, yes, you did."

I craned my head to the side as I took in the narrowed brown eyes of Mrs. Lawrence. The only orange cat at the library I was aware of was Rusty. Sure, he could get into trouble occasionally, but he was also lovable and lazy. What kind of harm could he have done to this lady to upset her?

"If you are talking about Rusty, he wasn't my cat."

"When Rose died, you took him, yes? Then you gave him to the library, which made him your cat for a period."

I rubbed at my chin as I mulled over her words. She was right. Rusty had stayed with me after his owner's demise, but it wasn't like I willingly let him crash at my home. The circumstances that had brought Rusty and me together were something I couldn't explain to another human being. Trying to explain that I could suddenly understand cats, one of the cat's my best friend charged me with watching was missing and an orange cat could help me find her, was impossible. I still had a hard time believing it and it was my life!

"You brought the orange cat here."

"Rusty," I said. The number of cats in my life was increasing all the time. If we didn't use their names, I was going to get confused.

"Rusty." The word came out stressed as she continued. "Is not a service animal, so he shouldn't be here."

"It's up to Mr. Tempest to decide if Rusty can be here or not."

Mrs. Lawrence turned back to the librarian, who looked like he wanted to be doing anything but be here at this very moment.

"If Rusty is allowed, then my sweet baby girl Peaches is too."

"It doesn't work like that."

"Why not? You think your cat is better than mine?"

I just stood there watching the two discuss what permitted Rusty to be here but not Peaches. Mr. Tempest wasn't budging on his decision, but I knew if this continued, he would either cave or it would blow up into something bigger. Against the better judgment of not wanting to get involved in things, I convinced myself to do so, as she was someone on the list I would need to question.

"Mrs. Lawrence," I said, making sure to keep my tone level. "I'm sure if your cat Peaches belonged to Mr. Tempest, then she would be allowed to stay, but it's a bit different. It doesn't mean we think less of her."

"It sure seems like you do."

Uh oh.

This wasn't going the way I'd hoped it would. It was time to change the topic.

"Do you spend a lot of time here?"

"A decent amount."

I nibbled on the bottom of my lip. What was a decent amount to her? Was she an avid reader who enjoyed spending most of her day here? Or was it more that she came here often enough in a month that it was decent?

"Like, daily?"

"Why does it matter how often I come? What matters is that Peaches isn't allowed to come with me and she comes everywhere."

I wanted to tell her I doubted she came to the grocery store, but here and now was not the time. I needed to stay on her good side to get some information from her and help save Mr. Tempest.

"Right, I was just wondering because if you came here daily, then maybe Rusty and Peaches could hang out to see if they could coexist in the library."

It was a lie, but she didn't have to know that. The final stay was with Mr. Tempest, and whatever he decided on didn't involve me. I already had three cats at home to care for, and adding two more was not in the plan.

"Not daily, more like every other week."

Every other week?

That wasn't even that often! She must be really attached to her cat that spending a few hours away two times a month was killing her. But when I thought about it, I couldn't judge her. Her situation was the opposite of mine, where I needed time away and she needed more time with them.

"Peaches is sweet and well-behaved. Unlike that orange cat who acts like he rules this place."

I snorted. Her glare quickly caused me to clap a hand over my mouth to stifle the next one. She may have a cat, but she didn't understand them, that was for sure. If only I could get her to meet Lola and understand her. She would know that cats were the boss, and we were just the minions.

"Just so you know, I will report this!"

I stiffened at her words.

"We don't need to go that far," I muttered, waving my hands in the air to calm the situation. "I didn't mean to laugh. It's just because cats can be bossy."

"Not my sweet Peaches."

She turned on her heels and stormed out of the library. All I could do was watch her leave. The information exchanged wasn't enough to tell me if she had a play in stealing the book and replacing it with a fake. But her displeasure with the library and Rusty was keeping her on my list of people I still needed to look into, that was for sure.

Chapter 9

After my run-in at the library with Mrs. Lawrence, I was more than ready to go home and relax. Sleep the rest of the day away to do it all over again. I tilted my head from side to side as I rubbed out the kinks that were settling. Solving a mystery was stressful work. It was one thing after another and I needed this moment to wind down.

Instead of shifting down the walkway leading to my home, I paused. A figure in the house's window next to mine had caught my attention. It was almost like she was beckoning me over; like she had a secret to tell. There was no mistaking the wide smile as she poked her head through the blinds. With a glance toward my house, I debated pretending I hadn't seen her. I was just a few seconds away from being able to relax, but the lady calling me over had been instrumental in helping me solve cases. Even if she'd roped me into a few of the cases herself.

Ignoring my need to hide away, I made the extra steps to the walkway leading to the Higgins home. Mrs. Higgins had already vanished from the window, seeing that she had caught my attention. I wasn't sure what she was up to, but I was about to learn fast. My knuckles rasped against the door as I waited for her.

"Kat."

Only it wasn't the lady of the home to greet me, but her husband. He stared at me with a cup of coffee in his hand.

"Afternoon."

"Heard you solving another case."

I nodded my head. Everyone in town had to know about my new status. Kat, the local crime-solving extraordinaire, who could talk to cats. Okay, maybe they didn't know the last part. That was something I was taking to the grave.

"You know what I tell you—"

"Oh, let her in, honey!"

The familiar voice of Mrs. Higgins filled the air, cutting off her husband's words, who could only grumble and step to the side to allow me entry into their home. As soon as I had passed the threshold, he quickly closed the door, took a sip of his coffee, and made his way back to the living room.

"I'm in the bedroom!"

There was no reason to continue the conversation with Mr. Higgins to figure out what his next words would be. I already had an inkling that it related to me roping his wife into my crime solving. If only he knew it was the opposite.

"How have you been, sweetie?" Mrs. Higgins called from the closet, her head poking out for a moment before disappearing.

"Good. I saw you wave to me on the street."

"That's right."

She reappeared once more, lugging a suitcase behind her before letting it fall to the ground with a loud smack in the center of her bedroom.

"Tell me the details of your—"

She tossed a look over my shoulder. One I couldn't help but mimic.

"Case. Sorry, didn't want the husband to hear," she whispered, with the biggest smile on her face.

"Well, there are several suspects," I said, only for her to raise a finger to her lips, letting out a soft hush. She patted the spot on the floor next to her, beckoning me over.

"Got to whisper or he will get suspicious."

"Won't he be even more suspicious if he doesn't hear us talking?"

"Possibly, but I will deal with that later."

I watched as she reached into the pile of clothes in the basket next to her, pulling out a skirt. Mrs. Higgins quickly folded the article and tucked it into the corner of the suitcase before repeating the action with a few more garments from the basket.

"Are you going on vacation?" I asked. I knew she was asking about my case, but I was more curious to hear about what was happening in her life.

"Yes, the husband is making me."

She let loose a sigh as her arms rested at her side, no longer folding the article resting on her lap. Mrs. Higgins turned toward me, still wearing that mischievous smile.

"He thinks a vacation will get me away from trying to include myself in the mysterious things around town."

It didn't seem possible, but I swear the smile on her face grew as she leaned in.

"Little does he know, I picked a cozy little town where crime is rising as our vacation spot."

I stared at Mrs. Higgins in bewilderment. Most people would go on vacation to escape the realities and harshness of the world. A place to get away from their responsibilities and just relax. Not Mrs. Higgins. A vacation was just the optimal time to dive right into more mysterious.

"He doesn't know, does he?" I whispered, thinking about the man who sat in the living room, who, no doubt, was still sipping away at his coffee, unaware of his wife's plans.

"Of course not."

"What's he going to do while you solve the crime?"

Mrs. Higgins returned to folding the clothes she had placed in her lap, neatly tucking them away before grabbing additional garments to put away.

"Solve them with me, of course."

Mr. Higgins solving crime again? Now that was something I hadn't expected to hear. Being a retired detective, he wanted to spend the rest of his years away from crime. Too bad he was in for a treat when he landed wherever they were going for vacation.

"Well, I can't wait to hear all about it when you return. How long will you be gone?"

"For the summer. Not too long."

She stopped folding, turning my way as she grabbed my hands.

"You've got to hold down the fort while I'm gone. You're being promoted from apprentice to master."

There was that big smile on her face once more. I had never asked to be roped into the crime that unfolded in my not-so-cozy town. But with talking cats and a neighbor who gravitated toward the mysterious things, it was impossible to stay away. Though being a master crime solver and the go-to person for others may be out of my wheelhouse. I was no longer ready to tackle the responsibilities that would come with it. I still needed help solving my own cases. How was I expected to do them on my own? Which reminded me, I had a case to solve. Ignoring

Mrs. Higgins' comment about my recent promotion at an unpaid job I hadn't applied for, I gripped her hands in return as I leaned in slightly.

"Speaking of crime, you know about the library?"

"Of course. Who doesn't know about the library and the missing book?"

I reeled back in shock, eyes wide as I looked at the mischievous smirk on the lady's face before me.

"You know about the book?"

"How do you think the library gained the book?"

What?

Mrs. Higgins wasn't just some random neighbor. She had her ear in everything.

"Just how many mysteries have you solved?"

Mrs. Higgins dropped my hands as she cupped her chin, adopting a thinking pose as she mulled over my words. "It's a little hard to say, but maybe nine hundred and eighty-two?"

A snort escaped as she joined me. That number was memorized and there was no way she was forgetting it.

"I plan to make it one thousand while on vacation."

I nodded my head, my chuckles still escaping. To think Mrs. Higgins thought I was ready to be a master when I was only on case number five. I had a long way to go to consider myself at the same level as her.

"Maybe we can add one more; the library. No one other than me and you seem to know about the mysterious hidden floor."

Mrs. Higgins leaned back, her back resting against the foot of her bed as she looked at me.

"Tell me what you got so far."

So I did. I spilled everything about my run-ins with the people Mr. Tempest had listed, spilling the details with every one of them, and made sure I left nothing out. Though she probably already knew the information I was telling her because she was just that good at what she did.

"And anything else?"

I nibbled my bottom lip. There was one more thing I could mention, but how could I go about talking about it without exposing me? Telling her I could understand cats was out of the question, but dropping the tidbit of information that I think a cat is involved couldn't hurt. Hopefully.

"This may sound weird..." I said, clearing my throat. "I think a cat is involved." I would need to find an excuse quickly if she asked why I thought so.

"And only one of your suspects has a cat."

"That's true."

"Start there. One cat may lead you to another."

There was a wiggle to her eyebrows like she knew something but wasn't letting on. But that would be impossible. She couldn't know about my ability to talk to cats. She probably thought I really like cats with how much I hung out with them.

"Okay, back to Mrs. Lawrence it is," I said as I stood up, my legs numb from sitting on them longer than expected.

"And Kat?" Mrs. Higgins called as she stopped me from leaving her bedroom. "Don't forget. Never rule someone out till the mystery is solved."

"Right. Will do. Thanks!"

Chapter 10

I walked down the street to the area where Delores Fuller and Mrs. Lawrence lived. After my talk with Mrs. Higgins yesterday, I'd promptly passed out right after making sure the cats were fed or Luna would have never let me hear the end.

"Kat!"

I turned to the voice, instantly seeing Daniel rounding the corner in his uniform. "Heading to the cafe early today?"

"No. I'm working on a case."

"Great! I'll tag along."

I raised an eyebrow as Daniel jogged over to where I stood on the sidewalk. Why was he so eager to help with a case? Most people would run the other way, especially after he'd tried to help me last time.

"You don't have work?" I asked as I pointed to the clothes he wore.

"We have a new hire I was supposed to train, but she called out. So I'm all yours."

He shot me a smile as he started walking, giving me no choice but to follow him.

"Where are we going?"

"To Mrs. Lawrence's house."

"Oh. You know about Peaches?"

I snorted at his words. Did I know about Peaches? Of course I did. I might not have met the cat, but I knew about her.

"She's nice, but a little weird."

His words caused me to stop walking as I stared at Daniel. "You met her cat?"

"Yeah, she sometimes brings her to the cafe even though it's not allowed. Susan just doesn't want to deal with it."

That sounded like the person we were going to see. We kept walking down the street, passing by the homes that were too far out of my range to ever be able to purchase. Everyone who lived on this block had some money to their name.

"It's that one right there," Daniel said as he pointed to the two-story house with a nice peach color and a white picket fence.

"I wonder if she named her cat Peaches because she lives in a peach house."

"It wasn't always peach. It used to be gray."

"So it's her favorite color," I said as we walked up to the gate, easily reaching over and unhooking the latch so we could walk up to the front door. Wasting no time, I got down to business by knocking on the door. Muffled words erupted from the other side for a moment, then the door jerked open.

"Daniel!" Mrs. Lawrence exclaimed as she reached forward, wrapping him up in a hug, then stepping back. Her gaze shifted toward me, and she said my name in a less than enthusiastic tone. "Kat."

"Good morning."

"What are the two of you doing together?" she said, her hands going to rest on her hips. But my attention didn't stay on her long as they shifted downward to the feline between her feet. It weaved in and out between the legs, letting loose a soft purr, its white coat leaving small strands behind on Mrs. Lawrence's pants, though it mixed with the random orange strand because of the orange on the face and tail of the cat.

"Pretty cat," I said as I watched Mrs. Lawrence bend down and scoop her pet into her arms.

"This is Peaches," she cooed, giving her cat a few quick pats before looking back to me. "The one you won't let into the library."

"I'm not the one preventing her into the library. I don't even work there."

The one who actually didn't want another cat in the library was Mr. Tempest, but I had to make sure she knew.

"Hey, Peaches," Daniel said as he bent down, running his fingers along the top of her head, electing a purr from her.

"I love the attention!"

I bit my lip as the fresh voice joined us. I couldn't let the others know I could understand what Peaches had said.

"Who's the friend?" Peaches asked Daniel, knowing he wouldn't be able to respond. She weaved away from Daniel to stand in front of me, her blue eyes focused on me.

"Hello there."

"Hi," I said.

"Oh, you are the human who can understand us! I have heard so much about you!" she said as she stood on her hind legs, her arms reaching up my leg, almost like she was begging me to pick her up.

"Peaches likes you, but then again, there isn't anyone she doesn't like," Mrs. Lawrence said as she scooped up the feline in her arms.

"What brings you to my wonderful home? Something that crazy cat signed you up for?"

I tilted my head, keeping my mouth shut as I thought over her words. What crazy cat was she talking about? Glancing over at Mrs. Lawrence, I wondered if Peaches was also talking about Rusty. Did they both have something against the orange tabby cat in the library? Now I would need to get her alone, so I could question her about her comment and involvement at the library.

"Mrs. Lawrence, can we come in?"

"So you can try to get me to drop the library issue?" she said, tucking Peaches in her arms.

"Her and that library. I swear it's a never-ending drama," Peaches said as she wiggled free from her owner's arm to jump to the ground. My gaze followed the feline, who took a few steps before looking back at me. "Are you coming?"

I couldn't just tell Mrs. Lawrence her cat had invited me into her home, so I invited myself to walk inside.

"I'm sure she wants us to follow," Daniel said as he rested a hand on Mrs. Lawrence's arm, who instantly lost all of her toughness.

"Of course! You're always welcome here!" she said, clamping a hand on Daniel's before walking in, but not in the direction Peaches had gone. Which left me still standing outside the threshold of her home with no human or cat in sight. I shrugged my shoulders as I stepped into her home.

"I'm just going to go to the bathroom real quick!" I called out to the two other people who had already left. Quickly closing the door behind me, I followed where Peaches had gone. Hopefully, Daniel would keep Mrs. Lawrence busy, so she didn't come searching for me. The last thing I needed was her finding me nowhere near the bathroom, as I didn't know where it was.

"Peaches!" I whispered as I bent down slightly, trying to find the white cat with orange on the face and tail. She couldn't have gotten far, but she could have slipped into a crack and then I would be screwed.

"Peaches!" I tried again, raising my voice.

"What? I'm right here," she said as I turned the corner into the kitchen to see her sitting on the island table.

"Oh, I thought you were on the ground."

"Cats can climb," she said dryly as she lounged on the island counter, licking her paws. "Have you brought me a treat?"

"Was I supposed to?" I said as I pulled out a chair and sat down.

"You don't visit the Queen without a treat."

"Queen?"

What is she talking about?

"Though I guess that crazy cat has been trying to claim my title lately. You should know."

Peaches stretched out her paw to rest on her face as she just laid in front of me. Silence settled between us as I waited to see if she would clarify exactly what she was talking about, but she didn't.

"What crazy cat?"

"Lola, of course. Who else."

I choked on my spit as I realized Peaches was talking about one cat under my care. Surely Lola wasn't going around establishing herself as head boss around town? I groaned as I rubbed at my temples. Who was I kidding? Of course she was. It was Lola. She'd quickly established her dominance over me and it would be only a matter of time before she did it to others, cats included. No one was safe from her.

"Do I even want to know what she's been up?" I asked.

"Are you going to get her to give up her claim to her title?" Peaches asked, her paw dropping from her face.

"I don't think I can make that cat do anything," I said honestly. There was absolutely nothing I could do to control that cat. She had me wrapped around her finger and nothing could be done.

"Then why are you here?" she said, bringing herself to a sitting position, almost reaching eye level with me.

"To ask about the break-in at the library."

"And what about it?"

"So you know about it? Do you have any information you can provide me?"

If a cat could raise their eyebrows, I would swear Peaches did.

"And why would I do that? What's in it for me?"

I scratched my head at her response. Couldn't she just be the lovely cat Mrs. Lawrence bragged about and provide the information without needing something in return?

"What do you want?" I sighed, slouching in my seat.

"Lola, to give up the title."

"Could you ask for something I can actually do?"

"If you can't do that, then we have no business together," she said curtly before stretching and jumping off the counter onto the ground.

"Seriously, there is nothing else I can do for you?"

"That is all I want."

I watched as Peaches padded away and out of the kitchen, but I couldn't let her get away. Jumping out of the chair, causing the legs to screech against the tile, I raced after the cat before she could disappear.

"Wait!" I called as I reached for Peaches, putting a hand on her, forcing her to stop and turn to look at me. "Surely you can give me a clue about the break-in? And I'll see about Lola."

"My human had nothing to do with it," Peaches said as she scooted out from under my grasp. "Tell Lola if she is coming for my title, she better watch out."

And with those parting words, she darted away to who knows where.

"There you are!"

I whipped around to see Mrs. Lawrence storming toward me, Daniel just a few steps behind her. His eyes were wide as he pointed toward the door.

"I can't believe you took this time to search my house! Are you trying to find something on me? Don't think whatever you found will be helpful."

I sidestepped the lady who thought I was out to get her as I positioned myself next to Daniel. He wasted no time, and wrapping his arm around me, turned us toward the door.

"Well, Mrs. Lawrence, it was a pleasure, as always, talking to you. We should do this again," Daniel said, keeping his tone sugary sweet as he escorted me out of hostile territory.

"Of course, Daniel! You are always welcome. But next time, leave her at home."

Chapter 11

"Leave me at home?" I said as I stomped down the street. "What does she think I am, a pet?" I groaned as I set my hands on my hips. "Ha! I'm a human, not a pet. You can't just leave me at home."

I swirled on my heels to stare at Daniel, who had stopped walking or he would have walked right into me.

"And does she think we live together? We aren't a couple!"

Daniel glanced away but showed no intention of joining me in my venting session.

"I'm glad we left. I don't think I could be in her presence for much longer," I said as I turned back on my heels to walk down the street. The sooner I put distance between her and me, the better.

"I think I'm going to head home."

"No longer interested in case?" I asked, casting a look over my shoulder to see Daniel was still stopped on the sidewalk.

"I just remembered I had things to take care of today."

I raised my eyebrows at the sudden change of heart. But if he had stuff to take care of, there would be no point in holding him up. He had already done enough by distracting Mrs. Lawrence so I could spend time alone talking to Peaches.

"Okay, then. I'll see you later."

"Yeah." He rubbed at the back of his neck. "I'll see you around. Bye, Kat."

Daniel walked in the direction we had just come. I stood on the sidewalk a little longer, watching him leave. I was sure he didn't live that way, but maybe he had to pick something up before heading home. Shrugging my shoulders, I continued in the direction I was heading. I would make a quick stop by the library, and once I did a bit of canvas, I would head home. Maybe see if Lola had stopped by so I could question her about what she really was doing when she was out and about the town.

"Oh Lola, why couldn't you be normal?" I groaned as I fisted my hair for a moment before dropping my arms to the side. I needed to stay focused. I would deal with Lola later.

Picking up speed, I hurried down the street toward the library. It didn't take me long to arrive at the building due to living in a small town. One of the wonderful perks of living here.

Running up the steps, I pulled open the doors of the building, or tried to as the doors were locked. Pressing against the frame, I peered inside to see if I could find Mr. Tempest, but couldn't see him behind the counter. Pulling away from the door, I looked up at the sun still in the sky. It was still daylight out. Why was the library closed? Trying once more, I tried to wiggle the doorknobs, but the door didn't budge. Mr. Tempest was gone, and the library was closed. Bounding down the steps, I looked both ways to see if anyone was looking at me before darting down the side of the building. Good thing Rusty had taught me how to break in to the library. Getting a running head start, I ran toward the window that was cracked. This time, I easily gripped the ledge and hauled myself into the building. Still not as graceful as the first time, I crashed on the floor in a heap.

"I'm not cut out for this," I groaned as I lay on the ground, looking up at the ceiling. I caught my breath before hauling myself up.

"Now, to see if anything has changed," I muttered as I crept forward into the library.

"Rusty?" I called, trying to see if the orange feline was anywhere in sight. I could use the extra help to figure out if there were any clues I had missed.

"Rusty, are you here?" I asked again as I peered down the aisle, but there was no orange cat in sight. "Where could you be?"

I continued looking down the aisle, trying to find any evidence of orange fur.

"Rusty, seriously, where are you?" I groaned, getting slightly frustrated that I couldn't find him. If he wasn't down any of the next two aisles, I would just head down to the basement floor on my own. I could solve this crime without the help of cats. Turning down one of the many romance aisles, I spotted a mass curled up on the floor. One too large and not as colorful to be Rusty.

"Hello?" I called as I crept toward the huddled mass. Had Mr. Tempest left something on the ground? Was this the reason the library had to be closed up early? I continued to step forward, being slow and cautious with every step.

"What is this?" I muttered as I poked the gigantic mass with my foot. My body grew rigid as the thing shook, unfurling into something longer and leaner. Into something that resembled a human. Too frozen to move, I watched this person pick themselves off the ground and take off running, their body crashing into mine as I fell backward. Books pressed against my back, and my head hit the shelf as the already dark library disappeared into a void. My head throbbed as I felt my body fall to the ground. The thundering steps of someone running away were the last thing I heard before the darkness claimed me.

Chapter 12

"Did you take a nap here?"

I curled up in a ball, trying to ignore the voice talking to me. Couldn't they see I was trying to sleep? If only they could leave me alone so I could continue to sleep in my bed. Which was a lot harder than I remembered.

"Hello?"

A paw landed on my face and didn't move. Wiggling my nose, I try to signal the cat that this wasn't the time. I wanted peace and quiet.

"Why are you on the floor?"

"I'm not on the floor," I groaned as I rolled over on a hard surface away from the cat. Maybe I was on the floor after all. I cracked open one eye and saw rows of books.

"Huh?" I muttered, sitting myself up. "I'm at the library?"

"On the floor," Rusty said as he trotted up to me and sat in my lap. "Why are you on the floor?"

"I don't know."

I scratched my head, trying to recall why I would nap on the library floor, of all places. If I was tired, I would have gone home to sleep on my bed, not break in to the library to take a nap. Wait... break in! I scrambled to my feet, causing Rusty to tumble out of my lap.

"Hey!"

"There was someone here."

"The only person here is you," Rusty said as he sat down on the ground, looking up at me.

"Maybe right now, but not earlier," I said as I faced the area where the person who had knocked me out had been curled up. "Someone was here." I pointed to the spot. "Then they got up and ran into me." I raised my hand to the back of my head. "And I got knocked out by bumping into the bookshelf."

"What now? It's almost night."

"Night?" I repeated, confused, as I glanced out the windows.

"Oh, no..."

This wasn't good. I had been out for far too long.

"I need to go."

"Go where?"

"I need to feed the cats."

Rusty stood up as he headed toward the window I had crawled in hours before.

"I might as well tag along."

I rolled my eyes at the orange cat, even though he was already out the window and outside. Of course, he would want to tag along for free food. There was nothing that could separate a cat and a good meal. And if I didn't hurry, I would find out from Luna just how badly she needed a good meal, since it was past her feeding time. Wasting no other time standing in the closed library, I crawled out the window to land on the ground. With a quick dust of the knees, Rusty and I made our way down the street to my home in silence.

People were out and about, getting ready for their night activities. They spared a few glances my way, most of them dropping to the orange feline trotting next to me, but no one said anything. My shoulders dropped at that notion. The sight of me with a cat was normal. No one was making a comment to ask why I was strolling around town with a cat. This was my life now.

"What's on the menu for tonight?"

"The usual?" I said, confused by the sudden question.

"You need to level up your cooking skills."

"I'm not making cat food from scratch," I said as I walked a little faster. The sooner he ate, the sooner he would stop asking me questions about why I still served cat food.

After several minutes, we finally arrived at the street I lived on. The sun was long gone as the moon shone in the sky.

"Expecting company?"

"Huh?" I said as I looked toward my house. Someone was standing at the door, their back to me. "I don't think so." I slowed my pace as we got closer to my home. Who would visit me at night? Surely it couldn't be the person who had knocked me out?

"Hi," I called as I stood on the sidewalk, not walking down the path leading to the front door.

"Kat!"

I relaxed, recognizing the voice of who had spoken.

"Daniel, what are you doing here?"

"I came to apologize for my abruptness early today."

"It's okay," I said, confused about why he would need to apologize for having things to do. Everyone got busy, and if he had plans, then there was no reason to feel bad.

"Can I come in?"

"Sure!" I stepped forward, grabbing the key from my pocket and inserting it in the door.

"You brought Rusty with you?"

I glanced down at the tabby cat at my feet as I pushed open the door.

"WHERE HAVE YOU BEEN?" a voice screeched as soon I cracked open the door.

"Is everything okay?" Daniel asked as I still held onto the doorknob of my home. Slowly, I turned to him as I mustered the strength to smile.

"Actually, can you wait out here? I'm just going to feed them real quick and pop back out."

"I don't mind helping you feed them."

"No, it's okay!" I said as I slipped into the house, ensuring Rusty followed me. I didn't need him staying outside and causing a ruckus because I had forgotten him like Luna.

"Where have you been?"

There was anger in her tone as I signaled to Daniel that I just needed a moment. With the biggest smile I could muster, I closed the door behind me and ran over to the kitchen.

"Do you not hear me?" Luna said as she ran after me. "You are late for dinner."

"I know," I whispered. "I got knocked out, but I'm working on the food."

I grabbed their bowls and placed them on the counter before going over to the cabinet to grab their food. As soon as I cracked open the first one, Zaira appeared like magic, waiting to be fed.

"I'm a wonderful cat and don't cause trouble. All I expect in return is to be fed."

"You caused that scene at the fish shop."

"I was helping you on a case."

I popped open another can as I continued filling up the bowls so I could feed the three hungry felines at my feet. Luna was a wonderful cat most of the time, she just wasn't allowed to assist with cases anymore after last time.

"Alright, here you go!"

I spun on my heels, balancing three bowls in my hands as I placed them down on the ground, one after the other.

"Now you are fed, I have to go."

No one responded. Now that I'd fed them, they didn't have an attitude anymore. Food really was the way to someone's heart. Stepping around the cats, munching away, I made my way back to the front door and stepped outside.

"Sorry about that," I muttered sheepishly as I locked the door behind me.

Chapter 13

"Was everything okay?"

I nodded my head.

"I heard you talking to someone."

And that was why I hadn't wanted to respond to his question verbally.

"The cats must be a handful for you to be talking to yourself."

I snorted. If only he knew just how crazy the cats drove me sometimes.

"Are we going somewhere in particular?" Daniel asked. I turned to him, staring into his eyes. His gaze was soft, and he had his eyebrows knitted together. He was confused. That made two of us.

"Well, I think I'm getting closer to figuring out my case, but I just need to figure out who was in the library earlier."

"Earlier? It's closed today."

"Exactly! Someone knocked into me and I passed out," I said nonchalantly as I felt a soft pressure on my upper arm. Fingers digging in, but not enough to cause pain, just enough to let me know they were concerned. I turned toward Daniel, whose face was screwed up in worry.

"You got knocked out?"

"It's no big deal. I wasn't out that long, and Rusty found me."

I could tell Daniel was still uncomfortable with my words, as his hand stayed on my arm a little longer before removing it. The frown staying on his face as he started walking. I followed after him as we walked down the street away from my home. The more crazy scenarios I ended up in because of the cases I was working, the more normal things were starting to feel. Though I did my best not to accept this as part of my life, it was forcing itself on me.

"Mr. Tempest provided four names of people who could be at the center of what happened." I started recalling the beginner details of the case. Four people I had run into at some point. Each with a different story that would make them seem like they weren't the culprit. But someone had to be. I stuffed my hands into my pockets as we continued to walk down the street. I wasn't sure of our destination, but something would eventually catch our eye.

"Whoever doesn't have an alibi for their whereabouts is the one we need to question."

"Who do we start with?"

That was a good question. Who would be the best person to start with? Finding the person on the first try would be fantastic, but I already knew my luck. It didn't exist. We would be going through everyone tonight and needed a head start.

"Trent, maybe? You guys are friends, so it would be easy to question him."

Daniel held up his hand, motioning for me to stop as I looked at him with an eyebrow raised. Had he come up with a plan on how to question his friend? I watched as he fished around in his pocket before pulling out his cellphone. In an instant, he dialed a number, putting it on speaker as the ringing filled the air. Now I was even more confused. I tried to mouth to him who he was calling, not wanting to say what I thought in case the person on the other line answered.

"Trent," Daniel said as my mouth dropped open. Quickly grabbing the phone from his hands, I hung up the call.

"You can't just call him. He'll just lie."

"I'm actually calling the restaurant to see if Trent is working tonight."

I handed the phone back, waiting to see how his plan unfolded. If it saved us a trip, then I was all for it. Daniel dialed the restaurant again, the ringing tone filling the air.

"Thank you for calling *Gregory's Grill*! How can I help you?"

Daniel cleared his throat as he brought the phone up to his lips, still keeping the device on speaker. "Yes, is Trent working tonight?

"I'm sorry! We aren't allowed to tell people the schedules of our employees."

Confused about how this was supposed to help us, I looked over at Daniel. He muted them before answering me.

"Safety reasons. There are a lot of weird people out there."

That made sense.

"It's Daniel from *Sweet Temptations*. I was trying to see if Trent was closing so we could do a food swap."

Food swap? I mouthed the words. What food were we supposed to be swapping with the restaurant?

"Oh! I didn't recognize your voice! He's working a double today. Let me ask if he wants to do the swap."

The lady on the end disappeared as holding music replaced her only for a moment before Daniel hung up the call.

"That confirms it wasn't Trent you saw at the library."

"How so?" I said, confused about how Trent's closing cleared him from being at the library. Daniel motioned for me to continue walking as he shoved the phone back into his back pocket.

"Who's next on the list?"

"We can try to find Thomas or Harrison? Only after you explain what just happened."

Daniel let loose a chuckle as he locked his hands behind his head. "If Trent is working a double, that means he wouldn't have time to go to the library. We barely get time to eat during a double."

If the lady who had answered the phone was telling the truth, it bumped him to the bottom of my list of suspects. When I'd first met Trent, he hadn't seemed like the person to break in to a library and steal a book, but taking Mrs. Higgins' advice to heart, no one was fully off the list till the crime was solved.

"So three people left. Thomas, Harrison and Mrs. Lawrence."

Finding Mrs. Lawrence would be easy. We knew where she lived, but we had seen her earlier this morning. If we suddenly just arrived for a second time in the same day, she would grow suspicious. That was the last thing we needed; the culprit catching onto what we know.

"I'm not sure where to find Thomas or Harrison. Maybe the gym for Thomas, but that would be a far stretch."

"Do they have anything in common?"

I thought over Daniel's words as we continued strolling the street with no actual destination. We were just letting our feet lead the way while our minds tried to find the missing pieces of the puzzle.

"The library."

"Then let's go there."

"We can't. It's closed," I said as I turned to walk in the direction of the library. Everything had started there, so why couldn't every-thing finish there? People had gathered outside the building when they heard the news of the break-in. With two people with unknown locations, they would have to come to us if we couldn't get to them.

"I got it!" I said as I broke out in a light jog, Daniel trailing beside me easily. One of us was more athletic than the other, and it showed. His breathing was even, a smile on his face like this was a walk in the park. I didn't even want to see what I would look like in a few minutes.

"We lay a trap," I muttered between catching my breath. "Everyone gathered at the library when they heard the news of the break-in. So let's gather everyone again."

"By breaking in?"

"What?" I said, coming to a stop, my hands resting on my hips as I caught my breath. "Why would we break in to the library?"

"Isn't that what you were talking about?"

"No!"

The laugh that escaped was half forced as I started back to the library. If Daniel and I broke into the library, I would have to show him how. Then he would question why I already knew how to break in to a library and for how long I had been doing it. If it was anyone else, they might conclude that I was playing the whole town. Pretending to solve the case, all the while, I had stolen the book. But this was Daniel. He would just be concerned that I had broken into a building without him being able to ensure my safety. What a weird guy.

"No breaking in. Maybe just a note on the door."

"People will ignore the note."

That was true. We needed a good reason for people to flock around the library, forcing the culprit to come out and see what was happening. There would be no way they would risk staying away. But what did the library have that could entice a crowd? The magical book was already stolen, so that was off the table.

"If you were in love with the library, what would you want?" I asked Daniel.

"The ability to check out unlimited books and no late fees."

"That would draw the library folks, but we need to gather others. The more people we have, the more likely the ones we are looking for will show up."

We arrived at the library, going up the steps to peer inside the building. Lights were still off from earlier, indicating no one was inside. Or at least no one we could see.

"We need to offer something else to get people to show up."

"Like what?" Daniel said.

I stared into the empty building. What would convince me and other people to show up to the library out of the blue? It had to be big. Nothing small like a gift card would do. It would draw a few people, but not enough. Something bigger was needed. Then, suddenly, it hit me. My reflection in the glass was staring at me as I watched my lips curl up higher and higher, because I knew exactly what would cause me to show up.

"A billion dollars."

Chapter 14

"Are you sure this is going to work?" Daniel asked as we examined our handy work.

Was I sure?

Not exactly, but I had a wonderful feeling. After collecting the supplies last night, which comprised a blank white sign and caution tape, we got to work setting up outside the library like something big had happened again. Only this time, there was a reward for a billion dollars.

We plastered a white sign with bright colorful letters on the front doors of the library. But the best part was the giant billion dollars in green; it would entice anyone passing by to stop by and see why money was being offered. To make it even more eye-catching, we laid the caution tape on the railing. There would be no way for someone to ignore all the signs in front of them.

"I think so. We just have to wait."

I bounced down the stairs, making my way to the side of the building where I sat under a tree. Now all we had to do was be patient and everything would fall into place.

"How long do you think we have to wait?"

"Hopefully not…" I paused, seeing a young girl run up the library steps to read the sign. She squealed with delight and then ran down the steps. "Long?" I said hesitantly, unsure of what she was doing. We really didn't need to wait long as she returned with her parents. They stood outside the library chatting as they pointed to the front of the building. It was a domino effect watching things fall into place. It started with one family, then several strangers joined them.

"That was faster than expected," Daniel whispered by my side, though I was sure none of the people in front of the library would pay attention to two people sitting under a tree.

"Should we go over there?"

I debated on answering as I examined the growing crowd. If the people we were searching for weren't there yet, they should be soon.

"Yeah, let's try to blend in," I said as I stood up, dusting the dirt from my pants. Adopting a casual walk, I strolled over to the crowd.

"Oh, what's going on?" I asked the first lady, who was talking to another person beside her. She pointed to the library doors but didn't stop to elaborate. It wasn't needed. The billion dollars plastered on the sign was enough of a giveaway of what had caught people's attention.

"What is the meaning of this?" Mr. Tempest yelled as he came running down the street. "Why is everyone in front of my library?"

He pushed through the crowd, the yellow caution tape being exposed to him now. His hand went to his chest as he clutched his shirt.

"Not again!" he shouted as he ran up the steps.

"Did you tell him about our plan?" Daniel whispered in my ear, his shoulder pressing against mine.

"I thought you were going to do that."

"It was your plan."

He had a point. It was a plan I had put together. But that didn't mean I was to inform Mr. Tempest of our grand scheme of trying to offer a billion dollars for the return of an ancient book.

"There is nothing to see!" Mr. Tempest shouted at the crowd. "Who did— Kat."

I felt his gaze lock onto me. It was obvious to him who had put the sign up. He knew I was working on the case, and I needed information.

"There are Thomas and Harrison!" Daniel said as he pointed in the direction Mr. Tempest was coming from. To get to them, I would have to pass the angry man who was upset with me for causing an unnecessary scene in front of his library. I would just have to show him all this was happening for a reason. I marched forward, setting my lips in a tight line. I was a girl on a mission and I had my suspects right in front of me.

"Kat!"

"Mr. Tempest! Why don't you join us?" I quickly said as I hooked an arm around his arm. My movement forced him to turn and join me on a brisk walk to where two boys stood close to the stairs, almost inching their way to get closer to the sign.

"I'm sorry I didn't tell you about this, but can you just play along for a moment?"

"A moment?"

"It won't take long, promise," I said as we stepped up to the boys. "Morning!" I said happily, grabbing their attention. Thomas offered me a nod in greeting as Harrison just stared at me.

"I see you're interested in the billion-dollar reward."

"So it's true," Harrison said softly as he shifted his attention to the sign on the door.

"Billion dollars for a missing book, huh?" Thomas said as he dug into his back pocket, pulling out the scavenger hunt book he was working on. "Guess I don't need this anymore. I got bigger fish to fry now." Thomas ran up the steps of the library and started inspecting the signs, picking up the corners to peer at the back, but making sure not to rip it off the door.

"What are you doing?" I asked, watching the man get to work.

"Looking for clues. Surely there would be clues. I can't solve this without clues," he said as he bent down, inspecting things. He lifted the doormat and, upon finding it empty, set it back down before moving onto the potted plants.

"What is he doing?"

"Looking for a book," I said.

"Kat, who are you talking to?"

I turned to the voice, a different one than had spoken a moment ago. I wasn't sure what I was expecting, but Mrs. Lawrence standing by my side wasn't it. But she wasn't the most shocking thing, for there was a fluff ball in her arms. A cat with an unmistakable orange face and tail.

Uh-oh.

Now the person who had asked me what he was doing made sense. It wasn't a person who had asked, but a cat.

"Mrs. Lawrence! Peaches! Odd seeing you here."

"Library been targeted again? Serves you right for not letting my sweet Peaches into the building," Mrs. Lawrence said happily as she scratched her cat's head. She was on cloud nine, even though another crime seemed to have unfolded at the library.

"I hope you talked to your cat about giving up the title."

I shot Peaches a glare. Why was she talking to me in public when I couldn't respond? Not wanting to focus on the cat talking to me, just in case I enticed her to keep responding, I focused on Mrs. Lawrence. Out of everyone on my list, she was the one who viewed the place in a negative light. The only one actively going after the library to ruin its name.

"Mrs. Lawrence, which reward interests you the most?"

"None of it."

Interesting.

She wasn't a die-hard reader who would be overjoyed with the ability to check out unlimited books with no late fees. She already had money, so she couldn't be as easily tempted by it.

"Mrs. Lawrence, do you like rare books?"

She gave me an odd look, letting her gaze drift to Daniel as she raised an eyebrow.

"What use do I have for a rare book?"

"That would be something you need to tell me," I said, not letting her get away from the questioning so easily. "Out of everyone here, you are the only one who doesn't like this place, but you keep coming back."

"Is it illegal to come visit a library? No."

She turned around, exposing her back to me as she stood beside me in a huff. This wasn't good. If she wouldn't tell me anything, I needed to find someone who could. I glanced around, trying to see if anyone could help us when I landed on Daniel. The lady next to me loved him. He would be my best bet. Hooking an arm around Daniel, I brought him close, almost tugging too hard that he had to balance himself before he sent both of us tumbling to the ground.

"Oh, okay! That's fine. I was just asking because Daniel is looking for a book club to join, isn't that right?" I asked sweetly as I laid a hand on his arm. All he could do was let out a hum in agreement. This piques Mrs. Lawrence's attention, who turned back around, her arm going out to occupy Daniel's other side. Which now left us two looking at each other.

"I would be more than happy to start a book club with you! We could meet up at the cafe."

"Why not the library?" I asked.

"Because I only plan to come here for a little longer and then I'm done with the library."

Biting my tongue, I lightly jabbed Daniel. With pleading eyes, I begged him to take over the questioning.

"Are you moving?"

"Of course not!" Mrs. Lawrence let loose a laugh. "I'm just trying to help my niece with something."

Niece?

What could she possibly need to do to help out her niece that involved the library? More importantly, what could it be that involved getting Peaches access to the building?

"It's a secret," Mrs. Lawrence said as she leaned in to whisper in Daniel's ear, "but I'll tell you."

And then the next part was too soft to hear. Despite just being a step away, she could lower her voice to a point it was concealed. Daniel shifted his arm, causing me to look down to see if he was giving me a sign, but there was nothing out of the ordinary.

"Oh! She's getting married, and she thinks he's cheating?"

My mouth dropped as Daniel blurted out her secret without a care. I peered over his shoulder at the other person hanging off him. She looked shocked that he'd repeated it aloud, but soon the wonder was wiped from her face and replaced with a smile. He could do no wrong in her books.

"Unfortunately. If only she'd met a man like you, then she wouldn't have to worry. I could set you up."

Daniel shifted in to me, trying to break the contact with Mrs. Lawrence. So I took over. He had been incredibly helpful in pulling out information from the lady intent on getting her cat on the building.

"But why press to have Peaches in the library?"

"So she can help me spy, of course."

The gears in my head ground to a stop as I repeated her words. Mrs. Lawrence was spying on someone who spent a lot of time in the library. The gears shifted again as I examined the crowd. Trent had been working the night I had run into someone, and he wasn't someone who liked to go to the library. My gaze shifted to Thomas, who was still looking for a clue. While he spent more time in the library, he was no stranger to voicing why he was doing something. If Mrs. Lawrence's niece had been dating him, she would have had her worries settled as he talked about the hunt pretty often. But he had mentioned he had a girlfriend, so it could be him. With that one tidbit of information Thomas had provided, he stayed on the list.

Then my gaze shifted to Harrison, who had been quiet. He was obsessed with the meaning of life and spent all his time reading books. It had started out as a desire to understand his girlfriend and then reading had turned into a passion. He was also a big book lover because he had created a book bouquet to propose to his girlfriend.

Wait, propose?

I dropped Daniel's arm as I stepped forward to the man who had jumped to the top of my list. Mrs. Lawrence had mentioned her niece was getting ready to marry. Harrison was getting ready to marry as well. This couldn't be just a coincidence. I stepped forward till I positioned myself next to my suspect, his gaze never leaving the sign on the front of the library.

"You did it. You have the book."

"I don't."

"But you did at some point?"

He didn't answer. I furrowed my brows as I took Harrison in. He was different from all the others who had committed crimes so far. He wasn't doing this to get back at someone. He actually loved books. Probably their biggest advocate outside the Tempest family. So why steal a book when it would be better protected with the people who had cared for it for ages?

"Do you know where the book is?" I asked softly as I placed a hand on his shoulder.

"I was trying to find out why she enjoys reading so much."

I knew this part of the story but stayed quiet, letting me talk.

"I was just looking, but then I figured out the meaning of life from it."

The mysterious book that Lola had been trying to get for her world domination had told Harrison about the meaning of life? Could it be that this book was actually magical?

"Then I couldn't give it up. Its knowledge has to be shared, starting with the love of my life."

I wasn't sure if he knew, but he'd confessed to taking the book. He had snuck down to the bottom floor, removed the book from the podium, and then removed it from the building.

"But how did you know?" Mr. Tempest stepped forward. "How did you know about the basement floor?"

"I saw an orange cat."

I took a step back at Harrison's words. There was only one orange cat that lived at the library, and that was Rusty. But there would be no way he would jeopardize his home for a human he didn't know. Then factoring in helping someone steal the book would have him invoking the wrath of Lola. No, something had to be missing. There was no way Rusty was involved. My gaze shifted to Thomas, who was still in another world trying to find his billions. Could he have an orange cat he never told me about?

Possibly.

I shifted to look at Mrs. Lawrence, who still stood beside Daniel. Could that be why she was so adamant about getting Peaches into the library because she knew Rusty was up to no good? But how would she know? She couldn't talk to cats. The only people who could understand them were me and other cats. Movement in her arms caught my attention as I zeroed in on the feline. A mostly white cat with an orange face and tail. My heart raced. Harrison might have only seen parts of Peaches and was unaware that she had a white coat but orange features.

Orange cat...

Peaches also didn't like Lola. She would have no problem stealing the book if it meant causing havoc in Lola's name.

Mr. Tempest shook his head from side to side as he wrapped an arm around Harrison.

"Books are wonderful things, but they can also be dangerous with the knowledge they contain. Let's go down to the station and explain everything to them. I'll do my best to keep the charges minimal."

Harrison offered no resistance as they turned away to walk down the street to the police station.

"That's the mystery? That's it?" Thomas said. At some point, he must have stopped looking for clues to eavesdrop on our conversation. But he was right. This wasn't a crazy mystery with an equally crazy culprit. This was a book lover who had started on the right path but had gotten lost along the way. Mr. Tempest would go easy on him.

I shifted away from watching the pair walk down the street to the orange cat still in Mrs. Lawrence's arms. I couldn't ask her why she'd done it. Not unless I got her alone. But if she wanted to play with fire, I knew an equally crazy cat who wouldn't back down from the challenge. I was going to be telling Lola about her.

As soon as she returned from wherever she had run off to.

***

Thank you for reading Abyssinian Arrangement, if you enjoyed it please leave a review!

You can find the next book Maine Coon Mayhem here:

https://www.irisleigh.com/home/cat-aunt-cozy-mystery/

Iris Leigh

Iris Leigh stumbled upon the genre of cozy mystery by accident. Since Iris is easily scared she does her best to avoid horror books, tv shows, and films. But dying for some type of mystery without all the suspense to make her heart burst from terror was when someone asked if she had ever read a cozy mystery. Now she has fallen in love with the genre and started to write to bring her stories to life.

If you want to stay in contact with Iris and learn about upcoming releases, make sure to sign up for the newsletter! You can sign up by navigating to her website!

Website: www.irisleigh.com

A Cat Aunt Cozy Mystery

MAINE COON
MAYHEM

IRIS LEIGH